THE REJ

D0059291

OTHER BOOKS BY PAUL AUSTER

Novels

The New York Trilogy (City of Glass • Ghosts • The Locked
Room) • In the Country of Last Things • Moon Palace •
The Music of Chance • Leviathan • Mr. Vertigo • Timbuktu

Nonfiction

White Spaces • The Invention of Solitude • The Art of Hunger •
Why Write? • Hand to Mouth

Poetry

Unearth • Wall Writing • Fragments From Cold • Facing the
Music • Disappearances: Selected Poems

Screenplays

Smoke & Blue in the Face • Lulu on the Bridge

Editor

The Random House Book of Twentieth-Century French Poetry •
I Thought My Father Was God and Other True Tales from
NPR's National Story Project

Translations

Fits And Starts: Selected Poems of Jacques Dupin • The Unin-
habited: Selected Poems of André du Bouchet • The Notebooks
of Joseph Joubert • A Tomb for Anatole (Stéphane Mallarmé) •
On the High Wire (Philippe Petit) • Vicious Circles (Maurice
Blanchot) • Translations • Chronicle of the Guayaki Indians
(Pierre Clastres)

THE RED NOTEBOOK

NOTEBOOK

True Stories

Paul Auster

A New Directions Book

Grateful acknowledgment is made to the following magazines in which the pieces of this collection originally appeared: *Granta* ("The Red Notebook" and "It Don't Mean a Thing"); *The New Yorker* ("Why Write?"); and *Conjunctions* ("Accident Report").

Book design by Erik Rieselbach

Manufactured in the United States of America
New Directions Books are printed on acid-free paper.
First published as New Directions Paperbook 924 in 2002
Published simultaneously in Canada by Penguin Canada Books, Ltd.

Library of Congress Cataloging-in-Publication Data
Auster, Paul, 1947–
The red notebook : (true stories) / by Paul Auster.
    p.   cm. — (New Directions paperbook ; 924)
ISBN 978-0-8112-1498-8
    I. Title.
PS3551.U77 R43 2002
813'.54—dc21   2002001926

New Directions Books are published for James Laughlin
by New Directions Publishing Corporation
80 Eighth Avenue, New York 10011

FIFTH PRINTING

Contents

For Carol Mann

THE RED NOTEBOOK

I

In 1972, a close friend of mine ran into trouble with the law. She was in Ireland that year, living in a small village not far from the town of Sligo. As it happened, I was visiting on the day a plainclothes detective drove up to her cottage and presented her with a summons to appear in court. The charges were serious enough to require a lawyer. My friend asked around and was given a name, and the next morning we bicycled into town to meet with this person and discuss the case. To my astonishment, he worked for a firm called Argue and Phibbs.

This is a true story. If there are those who doubt me, I challenge them to visit Sligo and see for themselves if I have made it up or not. I have reveled in these names for the past twenty years, but even though I can prove that Argue and Phibbs were real men, the fact that the one name should have been coupled with the other (to form an even more delicious joke, an out-and-out sendup of the legal profession) is something I still find hard to believe.

According to my latest information (three or four years ago), the firm continues to do a thriving business.

2

The following year (1973), I was offered a job as caretaker of a farmhouse in the south of France. My friend's legal troubles were well behind her, and since our on-again off-again romance seemed to be on again, we decided to join forces and take the job together. We had both run out of money by then, and without this offer we would have been compelled to return to America—which neither one of us was prepared to do just yet.

It turned out to be a curious year. On the one hand, the place was beautiful: a large, eighteenth-century stone house bordered by vineyards on one side and a national forest on the other. The nearest village was two kilometers away, but it was inhabited by no more than forty people, none of whom was under sixty or seventy years old. It was an ideal spot for two young writers to spend a year, and L. and I both worked hard there, accomplishing more in that house than either one of us would have thought possible.

On the other hand, we lived on the brink of permanent catastrophe. Our employers, an American couple who lived in Paris, sent us a small monthly salary (fifty dollars), a gas allowance for the car, and money to feed the two Labrador retrievers who were part of the household. All in all, it was a generous arrangement. There was no rent to pay, and even if our salary fell short of what we needed to live on, it gave us a head start on each month's expenses. Our plan was to earn the rest by doing translations. Before leaving Paris and settling in the country, we had set up a number of jobs to see us through the year. What we had neglected to take into account was that publishers are often slow to pay their bills. We had also forgotten to consider that checks sent from one country to another can take weeks to clear, and that once they do, bank charges and exchange fees cut into the amounts of those checks. Since L. and I had left no margin for error or miscalculation, we often found ourselves in quite desperate straits.

I remember savage nicotine fits, my body numb with need as I scrounged among sofa cushions and crawled behind cupboards in search of loose coins. For eighteen centimes (about three and a half cents), you could buy a brand of cigarettes called Parisiennes, which were sold in packs of four. I remember feeding the dogs and thinking that they ate better than I did. I remember conversations with L. in which we seriously considered opening a can of dog food and eating it for dinner.

Our only other source of income that year came from a man named James Sugar. (I don't mean to insist on metaphorical names, but facts are facts, and there's nothing I can do about it.) Sugar worked as a staff photographer for *National Geographic*, and he entered our lives because he was collaborating with one of our employers on an article about the region. He took pictures for several months, crisscrossing Provence in a rented car provided by his magazine, and whenever he was in our neck of the woods he would spend the night with us. Since the magazine also provided him with an expense account, he would very graciously slip us the money that had been allotted for his hotel costs. If I remember correctly, the sum came to fifty francs a night. In effect, L. and I became his private innkeepers, and since Sugar was an amiable man into the bargain, we were always glad to see him. The only problem was that we never knew when he was going to turn up. He never called in advance, and more often than not weeks would go by between his visits. We therefore learned not to count on Mr. Sugar. He would arrive out of nowhere, pulling up in front of the house in his shiny blue car, stay for a night or two, and then disappear again.

Each time he left, we assumed that was the last time we would ever see him.

The worst moments came for us in the late winter and early spring. Checks failed to arrive, one of the dogs was stolen, and little by little we ate our way through the stockpile of food in the kitchen. In the end, we had nothing left but a bag of onions, a bottle of cooking oil, and a packaged pie crust that someone had bought before we ever moved into the house—a stale remnant from the previous summer. L. and I held out all morning and into the afternoon, but by two-thirty hunger had gotten the better of us, and so we went into the kitchen to prepare our last meal. Given the paucity of elements we had to work with, an onion pie was the only dish that made sense.

After our concoction had been in the oven for what seemed a sufficient length of time, we took it out, set it on the table, and dug in. Against all our expectations, we both found it delicious. I think we even went so far as to say that it was the best food we had ever tasted, but no doubt that was a ruse, a feeble attempt to keep our spirits up. Once we had chewed a little more, however, disappointment set in. Reluctantly— ever so reluctantly—we were forced to admit that the pie had not yet cooked through, that the center was still too cold to eat. There was nothing to be done but put it back in the oven for another ten or fifteen minutes. Considering how hungry we were, and considering that our salivary glands had just been activated, relinquishing the pie was not easy.

To stifle our impatience, we went outside for a brief stroll, thinking the time would pass more quickly if we removed ourselves from the good smells in the kitchen. As I remember it, we circled the house once, perhaps twice. Perhaps we drifted into a deep conversation about something (I can't remember), but however it happened, and however long we were gone, by the time we entered the house again the kitchen was filled with smoke. We rushed to the oven and pulled out the pie, but it was too late. Our meal was dead. It had been incinerated, burned to a charred and blackened mass, and not one morsel could be salvaged.

It sounds like a funny story now, but at the time it was anything but funny. We had fallen into a dark hole, and neither one of us could think of a way to get out. In all my years of struggling to be a man, I doubt there has ever been a moment when I felt less inclined to laugh or crack jokes. This was really the end, and it was a terrible and frightening place to be.

That was at four o'clock in the afternoon. Less than an hour later, the errant Mr. Sugar suddenly appeared, driving up to the house in a cloud of dust, gravel and dirt crunching all around him. If I think about it hard enough, I can still see the naive and goofy smile on his face as he bounced out of the car and said hello. It was a miracle. It was a genuine miracle, and I was there to witness it with my own eyes, to live it in my own flesh. Until that moment, I had thought those things happened only in books.

Sugar treated us to dinner that night in a two-star restaurant. We ate copiously and well, we emptied several bottles of wine, we laughed our heads off. And yet, delicious as that food must have been, I can't remember a thing about it. But I have never forgotten the taste of the onion pie.

3

Not long after I returned to New York (July 1974), a friend told me the following story. It is set in Yugoslavia, during what must have been the last months of the Second World War.

S.'s uncle was a member of a Serbian partisan group that fought against the Nazi occupation. One morning, he and his comrades woke up to find themselves surrounded by German troops. They were holed up in a farmhouse somewhere in the country, a foot of snow lay on the ground, and there was no escape. Not knowing what else to do, the men decided to draw lots. Their plan was to burst out of the farmhouse one by one, dash through the snow, and see if they couldn't make it to safety. According to the results of the draw, S.'s uncle was supposed to go third.

He watched through the window as the first man ran out into the snow-covered field. There was a barrage of machine-gun fire from across the woods, and the man was cut down. A moment later, the second man ran out, and the same thing happened. The machine guns blasted, and he fell down dead in the snow.

Then it was my friend's uncle's turn. I don't know if he hesitated at the doorway, I don't know what thoughts were pounding through his head at that moment. The only thing I was told was that he started to run, charging through the snow for all he was worth. It seemed as if he ran forever. Then, suddenly, he felt pain in his leg. A second after that, an overpowering warmth spread through his body, and a second after that he lost consciousness.

When he woke up, he found himself lying on his back in a peasant's cart. He had no idea how much time had elapsed, no idea of how he had been rescued. He had simply opened his eyes—and there he was, lying in a cart that some horse or mule was pulling down a country road, staring up a the back of a peasant's head. He studied the back of that head for several seconds, and then loud explosions began to erupt from the woods. Too weak to move, he kept looking at the back of the head, and suddenly it was gone. It just flew off the peasant's body, and where a moment before there had been a whole man, there was now a man without a head.

More noise, more confusion. Whether the horse went on pulling the cart or not I can't say, but within minutes, perhaps even seconds, a large contingent of

Russian troops came rolling down the road. Jeeps, tanks, scores of soldiers. When the commanding officer took a look at S.'s uncle's leg, he quickly dispatched him to an infirmary that had been set up in the neighborhood. It was no more than a rickety wooden shack —a henhouse, maybe, or an outbuilding on some farm. There the Russian army doctor pronounced the leg past saving. It was too severely damaged, he said, and he was going to have to cut it off.

My friend's uncle began to scream. "Don't cut off my leg," he cried. "Please, I beg of you, don't cut off my leg!" But no one listened to him. The medics strapped him to the operating table, and the doctor picked up the saw. Just as he was about to pierce the skin of the leg, there was another explosion. The roof of the infirmary collapsed, the walls fell down, the entire place was obliterated. And once again, S.'s uncle lost consciousness.

When he woke up this time, he found himself lying in a bed. The sheets were clean and soft, there were pleasant smells in the room, and his leg was still attached to his body. A moment later, he was looking into the face of a beautiful young woman. She was smiling at him and feeding him broth with a spoon. With no knowledge of how it had happened, he had been rescued again and carried to another farmhouse. For several minutes after coming to, S.'s uncle wasn't sure if he was alive or dead. It seemed possible to him that he had woken up in heaven.

He stayed on in the house during his recovery and fell in love with the beautiful young woman, but nothing ever came of that romance. I wish I could say why, but S. never filled me in on the details. What I do know is that his uncle kept his leg—and that once the war was over, he moved to America to begin a new life. Somehow or other (the circumstances are obscure to me), he wound up as an insurance salesman in Chicago.

4

L. and I were married in 1974. Our son was born in 1977, but by the following year our marriage had ended. None of that is relevant now—except to set the scene for an incident that took place in the spring of 1980.

We were both living in Brooklyn then, about three or four blocks from each other, and our son divided his time between the two apartments. One morning, I had to stop by L.'s house to pick up Daniel and walk him to nursery school. I can't remember if I went inside the building or if Daniel came down the stairs himself, but I vividly recall that just as we were about to walk off together, L. opened the window of her third-floor apartment to throw me some money. Why she did that is also forgotten. Perhaps she wanted me to replenish a parking meter for her, perhaps I was supposed to do an errand, I don't know. All that remains is the open window and the image of a dime flying through the air. I see it with such clarity, it's almost as if I have studied photographs of that instant, as if it's part of a recurring dream I've had ever since.

But the dime hit the branch of a tree, and its downward arc into my hand was disrupted. It bounced off the tree, landed soundlessly somewhere nearby, and then it was gone. I remember bending down and searching the pavement, digging among the leaves and twigs at the base of the tree, but the dime was nowhere to be found.

I can place that event in early spring because I know that later the same day I attended a baseball game at Shea Stadium—the opening game of the season. A friend of mine had been offered tickets, and he had generously invited me to go along with him. I had never been to an opening game before, and I remember the occasion well.

We arrived early (something about collecting the tickets at a certain window), and as my friend went off to complete the transaction, I waited for him outside one of the entrances to the stadium. Not a single soul was around. I ducked into a little alcove to light a cigarette (a strong wind was blowing that day), and there, sitting on the ground not two inches from my feet, was a dime. I bent down, picked it up, and put it in my pocket. Ridiculous as it might sound, I felt certain that it was the same dime I had lost in Brooklyn that morning.

5

In my son's nursery school, there was a little girl whose parents were going through a divorce. I particularly liked her father, a struggling painter who earned his living by doing architectural renderings. His paintings were quite beautiful, I thought, but he never had much luck in convincing dealers to support his work. The one time he did have a show, the gallery promptly went out of business.

B. was not an intimate friend, but we enjoyed each other's company, and whenever I saw him I would return home with renewed admiration for his steadfastness and inner calm. He was not a man who grumbled or felt sorry for himself. However gloomy things had become for him in recent years (endless money problems, lack of artistic success, threats of eviction from his landlord, difficulties with his ex-wife), none of it seemed to throw him off course. He continued to paint with the same passion as ever, and unlike so many others, he never expressed any bitterness or envy toward less talented artists who were doing better than he was.

When he wasn't working on his own canvases, he would sometimes go to the Metropolitan Museum and make copies of the old masters. I remember a Caravaggio he once did that struck me as utterly remarkable. It wasn't a copy so much as a replica, an exact duplication of the original. On one of those visits to the museum, a Texas millionaire spotted B. at work and was so impressed that he commissioned him to do a copy of a Renoir painting—which he then presented to his fiancée as a gift.

B. was exceedingly tall (six-five or six-six), good-looking, and gentle in his manner—qualities that made him especially attractive to women. Once his divorce was behind him and he began to circulate again, he had no trouble finding female companions. I only saw him about two or three times a year, but each time I did, there was another woman in his life. All of them were obviously mad for him. You had only to watch them looking at B. to know how they felt, but for one reason or another, none of these affairs lasted very long.

After two or three years, B.'s landlord finally made good on his threats and evicted him from his loft. B. moved out of the city, and I lost touch with him.

Several more years went by, and then one night B. came back to town to attend a dinner party. My wife and I were also there, and since we knew that B. was about to get married, we asked him to tell us the story of how he had met his future wife.

About six months earlier, he said, he had been talking to a friend on the phone. This friend was worried about him, and after a while he began to scold B. for not having married again. You've been divorced for seven years now, he said, and in that time you could have settled down with any one of a dozen attractive and remarkable women. But no one is ever good enough for you, and you've turned them all away. What's wrong with you, B.? What in the world do you want?

There's nothing wrong with me, B. said. I just haven't found the right person, that's all.

At the rate you're going, you never will, the friend answered. I mean, have you ever met one woman who comes close to what you're looking for? Name one. I dare you to name just one.

Startled by his friend's vehemence, B. paused to consider the question carefully. Yes, he finally said, there was one. A woman by the name of E., whom he had known as a student at Harvard more than twenty years ago. But she had been involved with another man at the time, and he had been involved with another woman (his future ex-wife), and nothing had developed between them. He had no idea where E. was now, he said, but if he could meet someone like her, he knew he wouldn't hesitate to get married again.

That was the end of the conversation. Until mentioning her to his friend, B. hadn't thought about this woman in over ten years, but now that she had resurfaced in his mind, he had trouble thinking about anything else. For the next three or four days, he thought about her constantly, unable to shake the feeling that his one chance for happiness had been lost many years ago. Then, almost as if the intensity of these thoughts had sent a signal out into the world, the phone rang one night, and there was E. on the other end of the line.

B. kept her on the phone for more than three hours. He scarcely knew what he said to her, but he went on talking until past midnight, understanding that something momentous had happened and that he mustn't let her escape again.

After graduating from college, E. had joined a dance company, and for the past twenty years she had devoted herself exclusively to her career. She had never married, and now that she was about to retire as a performer, she was calling old friends from her past, trying to make contact with the world again. She had no family (her parents had been killed in a car crash when she was a small girl) and had been raised by two aunts, both of whom were now dead.

B. arranged to see her the next night. Once they were together, it didn't take long for him to discover that his feelings for her were just as strong as he had imagined. He fell in love with her all over again, and several weeks later they were engaged to be married.

To make the story even more perfect, it turned out that E. was independently wealthy. Her aunts had been rich, and after they died she had inherited all their money—which meant that not only had B. found true love, but the crushing money problems that had plagued him for so many years had suddenly vanished. All in one fell swoop.

A year or two after the wedding, they had a child. At last report, mother, father, and baby were doing just fine.

6

In much the same spirit, although spanning a shorter period of time (several months as opposed to twenty years), another friend, R., told me of a certain out-of-the-way book that he had been trying to locate without success, scouring bookstores and catalogues for what was supposed to be a remarkable work that he very much wanted to read, and how, one afternoon as he made his way through the city, he took a shortcut through Grand Central Station, walked up the staircase that leads to Vanderbilt Avenue, and caught sight of a young woman standing by the marble railing with a book in front of her: the same book he had been trying so desperately to track down.

Although he is not someone who normally speaks to strangers, R. was too stunned by the coincidence to remain silent. "Believe it or not," he said to the young woman, "I've been looking everywhere for that book."

"It's wonderful," the young woman answered. "I just finished reading it."

"Do you know where I could find another copy?"

R. asked. "I can't tell you how much it would mean to me."

"This one is for you," the woman answered.

"But it's yours," R. said.

"It *was* mine," the woman said, "but now I'm finished with it. I came here today to give it to you."

7

_____

Twelve years ago, my wife's sister went off to live in Taiwan. Her intention was to study Chinese (which she now speaks with breathtaking fluency) and to support herself by giving English lessons to native Chinese speakers in Taipei. That was approximately one year before I met my wife, who was then a graduate student at Columbia University.

One day, my future sister-in-law was talking to an American friend, a young woman who had also gone to Taipei to study Chinese. The conversation came around to the subject of their families back home, which in turn led to the following exchange:

"I have a sister who lives in New York," my future sister-in-law said.

"So do I," her friend answered.

"My sister lives on the Upper West Side."

"So does mine."

"My sister lives on West 109th Street."

"Believe it or not, so does mine."

"My sister lives at 309 West 109th Street."

"So does mine!"

"My sister lives on the second floor of 309 West 109th Street."

The friend took a deep breath and said, "I know this sounds crazy, but so does mine."

It is scarcely possible for two cities to be farther apart than Taipei and New York. They are at opposite ends of the earth, separated by a distance of more than ten thousand miles, and when it is day in one it is night in the other. As the two young women in Taipei marveled over the astounding connection they had just uncovered, they realized that their two sisters were probably asleep at that moment. On the same floor of the same building in northern Manhattan, each one was sleeping in her own apartment, unaware of the conversation that was taking place about them on the other side of the world.

Although they were neighbors, it turned out that the two sisters in New York did not know each other. When they finally met (two years later), neither one of them was living in that building anymore.

Siri and I were married then. One evening, on our way to an appointment somewhere, we happened to stop in at a bookstore on Broadway to browse for a few minutes. We must have wandered into different aisles, and because Siri wanted to show me something, or because I wanted to show her something (I can't remember), one of us spoke the other's name out loud. A second later, a woman came rushing up to us. "You're Paul Auster and Siri Hustvedt, aren't you?" she said. "Yes," we said, "that's exactly who we are. How did you know that?" The woman then explained that her sister and Siri's sister had been students together in Taiwan.

The circle had been closed at last. Since that evening in the bookstore ten years ago, this woman has been one of our best and most loyal friends.

8

Three summers ago, a letter turned up in my mail-box. It came in a white oblong envelope and was addressed to someone whose name was unfamiliar to me: Robert M. Morgan of Seattle, Washington. Various post office markings were stamped across the front: *Not Deliverable, Unable to Forward, Return to Writer.* Mr. Morgan's name had been crossed out with a pen, and beside it someone had written *Not at this address.* Drawn in the same blue ink, an arrow pointed to the upper-left-hand corner of the envelope, accompanied by the words *Return to sender.* Assuming that the post office had made a mistake, I checked the upper-left-hand corner to see who the sender was. There, to my absolute bewilderment, I discovered my own name and my own address. Not only that, but this information was printed on a custom-made address label (one of those labels you can order in packs of two hundred from advertisements on matchbook covers). The spelling of my name was correct, the address was my address—and yet the fact was (and still is) that I have never owned or ordered a set of printed address labels in my life.

Inside, there was a single-spaced typewritten letter that began: "Dear Robert, In response to your letter dated July 15, 1989, I can only say that, like other authors, I often receive letters concerning my work." Then, in a bombastic, pretentious style, riddled with quotations from French philosophers and oozing with a tone of conceit and self-satisfaction, the letter-writer went on to praise "Robert" for the ideas he had developed about one of my novels in a college course on the contemporary novel. It was a contemptible letter, the kind of letter I would never dream of writing to anyone, and yet it was signed with my name. The handwriting did not resemble mine, but that was small comfort. Someone was out there trying to impersonate me, and as far as I know he still is.

One friend suggested that this was an example of "mail art." Knowing that the letter could not be delivered to Robert Morgan (since there was no such person), the author of the letter was actually addressing his remarks to me. But that would imply an unwarranted faith in the U.S. Postal Service, and I doubt that someone who would go to the trouble of ordering address labels in my name and then sitting down to write such an arrogant, high-flown letter would leave anything to chance. Or would he? Perhaps the smart alecks of this world believe that everything will always go their way.

I have scant hope of ever getting to the bottom of this little mystery. The prankster did a good job of covering his tracks, and he has not been heard from since. What puzzles me about my own behavior is that I have not thrown away the letter, even though it continues to give me chills every time I look at it. A sensible man would have tossed the thing in the garbage. Instead, for reasons I do not understand, I have kept it on my work table for the past three years, allowing it to become a permanent fixture among my pens and notebooks and erasers. Perhaps I keep it there as a monument to my own folly. Perhaps it is a way to remind myself that I know nothing, that the world I live in will go on escaping me forever.

9

One of my closest friends is a French poet by the name of C. We have known each other for more than twenty years now, and while we don't see each other often (he lives in Paris and I live in New York), the bond between us remains strong. It is a fraternal bond, somehow, as if in some former life we had actually been brothers.

C. is a man of manifold contradictions. He is both open to the world and shut off from it, a charismatic figure with scores of friends everywhere (legendary for his kindness, his humor, his sparkling conversation) and yet someone who has been wounded by life, who struggles to perform the simple tasks that most other people take for granted. An exceptionally gifted poet and thinker about poetry, C. is nevertheless hampered by frequent writing blocks, streaks of morbid self-doubt, and surprisingly (for someone who is so generous, so profoundly lacking in mean-spiritedness), a capacity for long-standing grudges and quarrels, usually over some trifle or abstract principle. No one is more universally admired than C., no one has more talent, no one so readily commands the center of attention, and yet he has always done everything in his power to marginalize himself. Since his separation from his wife many years ago, he has lived alone in a number of small, one-room apartments, subsisting on almost no money and only fitful bouts of employment, publishing little, and refusing to write a single word of criticism, even though he reads everything and knows more about contemporary poetry than anyone in France. To those of us who love him (and we are many), C. is often a cause of concern. To the degree that we respect him and care about his well-being, we also worry about him.

He had a rough childhood. I can't say to what extent that explains anything, but the facts should not be overlooked. His father apparently ran off with another woman when C. was a little boy, and after that my friend grew up with his mother, an only child with no family life to speak of. I have never met C.'s mother, but by all accounts she is a bizarre character. She went through a series of love affairs during C.'s childhood and adolescence, each with a man younger than the man before him. By the time C. left home to enter the army at the age of twenty-one, his mother's boyfriend was scarcely older than he was. In more recent years, the central purpose of her life has been a campaign to promote the canonization of a certain Italian priest (whose name eludes me now). She has besieged the Catholic authorities with countless letters defending the holiness of this man, and at one point she even commissioned an artist to create a life-size statue of the priest—which now stands in her front yard as an enduring testament to her cause.

Although not a father himself, C. became a kind of pseudo-father seven or eight years ago. After a falling out with his girlfriend (during which they temporarily broke up), his girlfriend had a brief affair with another man and became pregnant. The affair ended almost at once, but she decided to have the baby on her own. A little girl was born, and even though C. is not her real father, he has devoted himself to her since the day of her birth and adores her as if she were his own flesh and blood.

One day about four years ago, C. happened to be visiting a friend. In the apartment there was a *Minitel*, a small computer given out for free by the French telephone company. Among other things, the *Minitel* contains the address and phone number of every person in France. As C. sat there playing with his friend's new machine, it suddenly occurred to him to look up his father's address. He found it in Lyon. When he returned home later that day, he stuffed one of his books into an envelope and sent it off to the address in Lyon—initiating the first contact with his father in over forty years. None of it made any sense to him. Until he found himself doing these things, it had never even crossed his mind that he wanted to do them.

That same night, he ran into another friend in a café—a woman psychoanalyst—and told her about these strange, unpremeditated acts. It was as if he had felt his father calling out to him, he said, as if some uncanny force had unleashed itself inside him. Considering that he had absolutely no memories of the man, he couldn't even begin to guess when they had last seen each other.

The woman thought for a moment and said, "How old is L.?," referring to C.'s girlfriend's daughter.

"Three and a half," C. answered.

"I can't be sure," the woman said, "but I'd be willing to bet that you were three and a half the last time you saw your father. I say that because you love L. so much. Your identification with her is very strong, and you're reliving your life through her."

Several days after that, there was a reply from Lyon— a warm and perfectly gracious letter from C.'s father. After thanking C. for the book, he went on to tell him how proud he was to learn that his son had grown up to become a writer. By pure coincidence, he added, the package had been mailed on his birthday, and he was moved by the symbolism of the gesture.

None of this tallied with the stories C. had heard throughout his childhood. According to his mother, his father was a monster of selfishness who had walked out on her for a "slut" and had never wanted anything to do with his son. C. had believed these stories, and therefore he had shied away from any contact with his father. Now, on the strength of this letter, he no longer knew what to believe.

He decided to write back. The tone of his response was guarded, but nevertheless it was a response. Within days he received another reply, and this second letter was just as warm and gracious as the first had been. C. and his father began a correspondence. It went on for a month or two, and eventually C. began to consider traveling down to Lyon to meet his father face to face.

Before he could make any definite plans, he received a letter from his father's wife informing him that his father was dead. He had been in ill health for the past several years, she wrote, but the recent exchange of letters with C. had given him great happiness, and his last days had been filled with optimism and joy.

It was at this moment that I first heard about the incredible reversals that had taken place in C.'s life. Sitting on the train from Paris to Lyon (on his way to visit his "stepmother" for the first time), he wrote me a letter that sketched out the story of the past month. His handwriting reflected each jolt of the tracks, as if the speed of the train were an exact image of the thoughts racing through his head. As he put it somewhere in that letter: "I feel as if I've become a character in one of your novels."

His father's wife could not have been friendlier to him during that visit. Among other things, C. learned that his father had suffered a heart attack on the morning of his last birthday (the same day that C. had looked up his address on the *Minitel*) and that, yes, C. had been precisely three and a half years old at the time of his parents' divorce. His stepmother then went on to tell him the story of his life from his father's point of view—which contradicted everything his mother had ever told him. In this version, it was his mother who had walked out on his father; it was his mother who had forbidden his father from seeing him; it was his mother who had broken his father's heart. She told C. how his father would come around to the schoolyard when he was a little boy to look at him through the fence. C. remembered that man, but not knowing who he was, he had been afraid.

C.'s life had now become two lives. There was Version A and Version B, and both of them were his story. He had lived them both in equal measure, two truths that canceled each other out, and all along, without even knowing it, he had been stranded in the middle.

His father had owned a small stationery store (the usual stock of paper and writing materials, along with a rental library of popular books). The business had earned him a living, but not much more than that, and the estate he left behind was quite modest. The numbers are unimportant, however. What counts is that C.'s stepmother (by then an old woman) insisted on splitting the money with him half and half. There was nothing in the will that required her to do that, and morally speaking she needn't have parted with a single penny of her husband's savings. She did it because she wanted to, because it made her happier to share the money than to keep it for herself.

IO

In thinking about friendship, particularly about how some friendships endure and others don't, I am reminded of the fact that in all my years of driving I have had just four flat tires, and that on each of these occasions the same person was in the car with me (in three different countries, spread out over a period of eight or nine years). J. was a college friend, and though there was always an edge of unease and conflict in our relations, for a time we were close. One spring while we were still undergraduates, we borrowed my father's ancient station wagon and drove up into the wilderness of Quebec. The seasons change more slowly in that part of the world, and winter was not yet over. The first flat tire did not present a problem (we were equipped with a spare), but when a second tire blew out less than an hour later, we were stranded in the bleak and frigid countryside for most of the day. At the time, I shrugged off the incident as a piece of bad luck, but four or five years later, when

J. came to France to visit the house where L. and I were working as caretakers (in miserable condition, inert with depression and self-pity, unaware that he was overstaying his welcome with us), the same thing happened. We went to Aix-en-Provence for the day (a drive of about two hours), and coming back later that night on a dark, back-country road, we had another flat. Just a coincidence, I thought, and then pushed the event out of my mind. But then, four years after that, in the waning months of my marriage to L., J. came to visit us again—this time in New York State, where L. and I were living with the infant Daniel. At one point, J. and I climbed into the car to go to the store and shop for dinner. I pulled the car out of the garage, turned it around in the rutted dirt driveway, and advanced to the edge of the road to look left, right, and left before going on. Just then, as I waited for a car to pass by, I heard the unmistakable hiss of escaping air. Another tire had gone flat, and this time we hadn't even left the house. J. and I both laughed, of course, but the truth is that our friendship never really recovered from that fourth flat tire. I'm not saying that the flat tires were responsible for our drifting apart, but in some perverse way they were an emblem of how things had always stood between us, the sign of some impalpable curse. I don't want to exaggerate, but even now I can't quite bring myself to reject those flat tires as meaningless. For the fact is that J. and I have lost contact, and we have not spoken to each other in more than ten years.

II

In 1990, I found myself in Paris again for a few days. One afternoon, I stopped by the office of a friend to say hello and was introduced to a Czech woman in her late forties or early fifties—an art historian who happened to be a friend of my friend. She was an attractive and vivacious person, I remember, but since she was on the point of leaving when I walked in, I spent no more than five or ten minutes in her company. As usually happens in such situations, we talked about nothing of any importance: a town we both knew in America, the subject of a book she was reading, the weather. Then we shook hands, she walked out the door, and I have never seen her again.

After she was gone, the friend I had come to visit leaned back in her chair and said, "Do you want to hear a good story?"

"Of course," I said, "I'm always interested in good stories."

"I like my friend very much," she continued, "so don't get the wrong idea. I'm not trying to spread

48

gossip about her. It's just that I feel you have a right to know this."

"Are you sure?"

"Yes, I'm sure. But you have to promise me one thing. If you ever write the story, you mustn't use anyone's name."

"I promise," I said.

And so my friend let me in on the secret. From start to finish, it couldn't have taken her more than three minutes to tell the story I am about to tell now.

The woman I had just met was born in Prague during the war. When she was still a baby, her father was captured, impressed into the German army, and shipped off to the Russian front. She and her mother never heard from him again. They received no letters, no news to tell them if he was alive or dead, nothing. The war just swallowed him up, and he vanished without a trace.

Years passed. The girl grew up. She completed her studies at the university and became a professor of art history. According to my friend, she ran into trouble with the government during the Soviet crackdown in the late sixties, but exactly what kind of trouble was never made clear to me. Given the stories I know about what happened to other people during that time, it is not very difficult to guess.

At some point, she was allowed to begin teaching

again. In one of her classes, there was an exchange student from East Germany. She and this young man fell in love, and eventually they were married.

Not long after the wedding, a telegram arrived announcing the death of her husband's father. The next day, she and her husband traveled to East Germany to attend the funeral. Once there, in whatever town or city it was, she learned that her now dead father-in-law had been born in Czechoslovakia. During the war he had been captured by the Nazis, impressed into the German army, and shipped off to the Russian front. By some miracle, he had managed to survive. Instead of returning to Czechoslovakia after the war, however, he had settled in Germany under a new name, had married a German woman, and had lived there with his new family until the day of his death. The war had given him a chance to start all over again, and it seems that he had never looked back.

When my friend's friend asked what this man's name had been in Czechoslovakia, she understood that he was her father.

Which meant, of course, that insofar as her husband's father was the same man, the man she had married was also her brother.

12

One afternoon many years ago, my father's car stalled at a red light. A terrible storm was raging, and at the exact moment his engine went dead, lightning struck a large tree by the side of the road. The trunk of the tree split in two, and as my father struggled to get the car started again (unaware that the upper half of the tree was about to fall), the driver of the car behind him, seeing what was about to happen, put his foot on the accelerator and pushed my father's car through the intersection. An instant later, the tree came crashing to the ground, landing in the very spot where my father's car had just been. What was very nearly the end of him proved to be no more than a close call, a brief episode in the ongoing story of his life.

A year or two after that, my father was working on the roof of a building in Jersey City. Somehow or other (I wasn't there to witness it), he slipped off the edge and started falling to the ground. Once again he was headed for certain disaster, and once again he was saved. A clothesline broke his fall, and he walked away from the accident with only a few bumps and bruises. Not even a concussion. Not a single broken bone.

That same year, our neighbors across the street hired two men to paint their house. One of the workers fell off the roof and was killed.

The little girl who lived in that house happened to be my sister's best friend. One winter night, the two of them went to a costume party (they were six or seven years old, and I was nine or ten). It had been arranged that my father would pick them up after the party, and when the time came I went along to keep him company in the car. It was bitter cold that night, and the roads were covered with treacherous sheets of ice. My father drove carefully, and we made the journey back and forth without incident. As we pulled up in front of the girl's house, however, a number of unlikely events occurred all at once.

My sister's friend was dressed as a fairy princess. To complete the outfit, she had borrowed a pair of her mother's high heels, and because her feet swam in those shoes, every step she took was turned into an adventure. My father stopped the car and climbed out to accompany her to the front door. I was in the back with the girls, and in order to let my sister's friend out, I had to get out first. I remember standing on the curb as she disentangled herself from the seat, and just as she stepped into the open air, I noticed that the car was rolling slowly in reverse—either because of the ice or because my father had forgotten to engage the emergency brake (I don't know)—but before I could tell my father what was happening, my sister's friend touched the curb with her mother's high heels and slipped. She went skidding under the car—which was still moving—and there she was, about to be crushed to death by the wheels of my father's Chevy. As I remember it, she didn't make a sound. Without pausing to think, I bent down from the curb, grabbed hold of her right hand, and in one quick gesture yanked her to the sidewalk. An instant later, my father finally noticed that the car was moving. He jumped back into the driver's seat, stepped on the brake, and brought the machine to a halt. From start to finish, the whole chain of misadventures couldn't have taken more than eight or ten seconds.

For years afterward, I walked around feeling that this had been my finest moment. I had actually saved someone's life, and in retrospect I was always astonished by how quickly I had acted, by how sure my movements had been at the critical juncture. I saw the rescue in my mind again and again; again and again I relived the sensation of pulling that little girl out from under the car.

About two years after that night, our family moved to another house. My sister fell out of touch with her friend, and I myself did not see her for another fifteen years.

It was June, and my sister and I had both come back to town for a short visit. Just by chance, her old friend dropped by to say hello. She was all grown up now, a young woman of twenty-two who had graduated from college earlier that month, and I must say that I felt some pride in seeing that she had made it to adulthood in one piece. In a casual sort of way, I mentioned the night I had pulled her out from under the car. I was curious to know how well she remembered her brush with death, but from the look on her face when I asked the question, it was clear that she remembered nothing. A blank stare. A slight frown. A shrug. She remembered nothing!

I realized then that she hadn't known the car was moving. She hadn't even known that she was in danger. The whole incident had taken place in a flash: ten seconds of her life, an interval of no account, and none of it had left the slightest mark on her. For me, on the other hand, those seconds had been a defining experience, a singular event in my internal history.

Most of all, it stuns me to acknowledge that I am talking about something that happened in 1956 or 1957—and that the little girl of that night is now over forty years old.

13

My first novel was inspired by a wrong number. I was alone in my apartment in Brooklyn one afternoon, sitting at my desk and trying to work when the telephone rang. If I am not mistaken, it was the spring of 1980, not many days after I found the dime outside Shea Stadium.

I picked up the receiver, and the man on the other end asked if he was talking to the Pinkerton Agency. I told him no, he had dialed the wrong number, and hung up. Then I went back to work and promptly forgot about the call.

The next afternoon, the telephone rang again. It turned out to be the same person asking the same question I had been asked the day before: "Is this the Pinkerton Agency?" Again I said no, and again I hung up. This time, however, I started thinking about what would have happened if I had said yes. What if I had pretended to be a detective from the Pinkerton Agency? I wondered. What if I had actually taken on the case?

To tell the truth, I felt that I had squandered a rare opportunity. If the man ever called again, I told myself, I would at least talk to him a little bit and try to find out what was going on. I waited for the telephone to ring again, but the third call never came.

After that, wheels started turning in my head, and little by little an entire world of possibilities opened up to me. When I sat down to write *City of Glass* a year later, the wrong number had been transformed into the crucial event of the book, the mistake that sets the whole story in motion. A man named Quinn receives a phone call from someone who wants to talk to Paul Auster, the private detective. Just as I did, Quinn tells the caller he has dialed the wrong number. It happens again on the next night, and again Quinn hangs up. Unlike me, however, Quinn is given another chance. When the phone rings again on the third night, he plays along with the caller and takes on the case. Yes, he says, I'm Paul Auster—and at that moment the madness begins.

Most of all, I wanted to remain faithful to my original impulse. Unless I stuck to the spirit of what had really happened, I felt there wouldn't have been any purpose to writing the book. That meant implicating myself in the action of the story (or at least someone who resembled me, who bore my name), and it also meant writing about detectives who were not detectives, about impersonation, about mysteries that cannot be solved. For better or worse, I felt I had no choice.

All well and good. I finished the book ten years ago, and since then I have gone on to occupy myself with other projects, other ideas, other books. Less than two months ago, however, I learned that books are never finished, that it is possible for stories to go on writing themselves without an author.

I was alone in my apartment in Brooklyn that after-noon, sitting at my desk and trying to work when the telephone rang. This was a different apartment from the one I had in 1980—a different apartment with a different telephone number. I picked up the receiver, and the man on the other end asked if he could speak to Mr. Quinn. He had a Spanish accent and I did not recognize the voice. For a moment I thought it might be one of my friends trying to pull my leg. "Mr. Quinn?" I said. "Is this some kind of joke or what?"

No, it wasn't a joke. The man was in dead earnest. He had to talk to Mr. Quinn, and would I please put him on the line. Just to make sure, I asked him to spell out the name. The caller's accent was quite thick, and I was hoping that he wanted to talk to Mr. Queen. But no such luck. "Q-U-I-N-N," the man answered. I suddenly grew scared, and for a moment or two I couldn't get any words out of my mouth. "I'm sorry," I said at last, "there's no Mr. Quinn here. You've dialed the wrong number." The man apologized for disturbing me, and then we both hung up.

This really happened. Like everything else I have set down in this red notebook, it is a true story.

1992

WHY WRITE?

I

A German friend tells of the circumstances that preceded the births of her two daughters.

Nineteen years ago, hugely pregnant and already several weeks past due, A. sat down on the sofa in her living room and turned on the television set. As luck would have it, the opening credits of a film were just coming on screen. It was *The Nun's Story*, a 1950s Hollywood drama starring Audrey Hepburn. Glad for the distraction, A. settled in to watch the movie and immediately got caught up in it. Halfway through, she went into labor. Her husband drove her to the hospital, and she never learned how the film turned out.

Three years later, pregnant with her second child, A. sat down on the sofa and turned on the television set once again. Once again a film was playing, and once again it was *The Nun's Story* with Audrey Hepburn. Even more remarkable (and A. was very emphatic about this point), she had tuned in to the film at the precise moment where she had left off three years earlier. This time she was able to see the film through to the end. Less than fifteen minutes later, her water broke, and she went off to the hospital to give birth for the second time.

These two daughters are A.'s only children. The first labor was extremely difficult (my friend nearly didn't make it and was ill for many months afterward), but the second delivery went smoothly, with no complications of any kind.

2

Five years ago, I spent the summer with my wife and children in Vermont, renting an old, isolated farmhouse on the top of a mountain. One day, a woman from the next town stopped by to visit with her two children, a girl of four and a boy of eighteen months. My daughter Sophie had just turned three, and she and the girl enjoying playing with each other. My wife and I sat down in the kitchen with our guest, and the children ran off to amuse themselves.

Five minutes later, there was a loud crash. The little boy had wandered into the front hall at the other end of the house, and since my wife had put a vase of flowers in that hall just two hours earlier, it wasn't difficult to guess what had happened. I didn't even have to look to know that the floor was covered with broken glass and pools of water—along with the stems and petals of a dozen scattered flowers.

I was annoyed. Goddamn kids, I said to myself. Goddamn people with their goddamn clumsy kids. Who gave them the right to drop by without calling first?

I told my wife that I'd clean up the mess, and so while she and our visitor continued their conversation, I gathered up a broom, a dustpan, and some towels and marched off to the front of the house.

My wife had put the flowers on a wooden trunk that sat just below the staircase railing. This staircase was especially steep and narrow, and there was a large window not more than a yard from the bottom step. I mention this geography because it's important. Where things were has everything to do with what happened next.

I was about half finished with the clean-up job when my daughter rushed out from her room onto the second-floor landing. I was close enough to the foot of the stairs to catch a glimpse of her (a couple of steps back and she would have been blocked from view), and in that brief moment I saw that she had that high-spirited, utterly happy expression on her face that has filled my middle age with such overpowering gladness. Then, an instant later, before I could even say hello, she tripped. The toe of her sneaker had caught on the landing, and just like that, without any cry or warning, she was sailing through the air. I don't mean to suggest that she was falling or tumbling or bouncing down the steps. I mean to say that she was flying. The impact of the stumble had literally launched her into space, and from the trajectory of her flight I could see that she was heading straight for the window.

What did I do? I don't know what I did. I was on the wrong side of the banister when I saw her trip, but by the time she was midway between the landing and the window, I was standing on the bottom step of the staircase. How did I get there? It was no more than a question of several feet, but it hardly seems possible to cover that distance in that amount of time—which is next to no time at all. Nevertheless, I was there, and the moment I got there I looked up, opened my arms, and caught her.

3

I was fourteen. For the third year in a row, my parents had sent me to a summer camp in New York State. I spent the bulk of my time playing basketball and baseball, but as it was a co-ed camp, there were other activities as well: evening "socials," the first awkward grapplings with girls, panty raids, the usual adolescent shenanigans. I also remember smoking cheap cigars on the sly, "frenching" beds, and massive water-balloon fights.

None of this is important. I simply want to underscore what a vulnerable age fourteen can be. No longer a child, not yet an adult, you bounce back and forth between who you were and who you are about to become. In my own case, I was still young enough to think that I had a legitimate shot at playing in the Major Leagues, but old enough to be questioning the existence of God. I had read the Communist Manifesto, and yet I still enjoyed watching Saturday morning cartoons. Every time I saw my face in the mirror, I seemed to be looking at someone else.

There were sixteen or eighteen boys in my group. Most of us had been together for several years, but a couple of newcomers had also joined us that summer. One was named Ralph. He was a quiet kid without much enthusiasm for dribbling basketballs or hitting the cut-off man, and while no one gave him a particularly hard time, he had trouble blending in. He had flunked a couple of subjects that year, and most of his free periods were spent being tutored by one of the counselors. It was a little sad, and I felt sorry for him—but not too sorry, not sorry enough to lose any sleep over it.

Our counselors were all New York college students from Brooklyn and Queens. Wise-cracking basketball players, future dentists, accountants, and teachers, city kids to their very bones. Like most true New Yorkers, they persisted in calling the ground the "floor," even when all that was under their feet was grass, pebbles, and dirt. The trappings of traditional summer camp life were as alien to them as the I.R.T. is to an Iowa farmer. Canoes, lanyards, mountain climbing, pitching tents, singing around the campfire were nowhere to be found in the inventory of their concerns. They could drill us on the finer points of setting picks and boxing out for rebounds, but otherwise they mostly horsed around and told jokes.

Imagine our surprise, then, when one afternoon

our counselor announced that we were going for a hike in the woods. He had been seized by an inspiration and wasn't going to let anyone talk him out of it. Enough basketball, he said. We're surrounded by nature, and it's time we took advantage of it and started acting like real campers—or words to that effect. And so, after the rest period that followed lunch, the whole gang of sixteen or eighteen boys along with two or three counselors set off into the woods.

It was late July, 1961. Everyone was in a fairly buoyant mood, I remember, and half an hour or so into the trek most people agreed that the outing had been a good idea. No one had a compass, of course, or the slightest clue as to where we were going, but we were all enjoying ourselves, and if we happened to get lost, what difference would that make? Sooner or later, we'd find our way back.

Then it began to rain. At first it was barely noticeable, a few light drops falling between the leaves and branches, nothing to worry about. We walked on, unwilling to let a little water spoil our fun, but a couple of minutes later it started coming down in earnest. Everyone got soaked, and the counselors decided we should turn around and head back. The only problem was that no one knew where the camp was. The woods were thick, dense with clusters of trees and thorn-studded bushes, and we had woven our way this way and that, abruptly shifting directions in order to move on. To add to the confusion, it was becoming hard to see. The woods were dark to begin with, but with the rain falling and the sky turning black, it felt more like night than three or four in the afternoon.

Then the thunder started. And after the thunder, the lightning started. The storm was directly on top of us, and it turned out to be the summer storm to end all summer storms. I have never seen weather like that before or since. The rain poured down on us so hard that it actually hurt; each time the thunder exploded, you could feel the noise vibrating inside your body. Immediately after that, the lightning would come, dancing around us like spears. It was as if weapons had materialized out of thin air: a sudden flash that turned everything a bright, ghostly white. Trees were struck, and the branches would begin to smolder. Then it would go dark again for a moment, there would be another crash in the sky, and the lightning would return in a different spot.

The lightning was what scared us, of course. It would have been stupid not to be scared, and in our panic we tried to run away from it. But the storm was too big, and everywhere we went we were met by more lightning. It was a helter-skelter stampede, a headlong rush in circles. Then, suddenly, someone spotted a clearing in the woods. A brief dispute broke out over whether it was safer to go into the open or continue to stand under the trees. The voice arguing for the open won, and we all ran in the direction of the clearing.

It was a small meadow, most likely a pasture that belonged to a local farm, and to get to it we had to crawl under a barbed-wire fence. One by one, we got down on our bellies and inched our way through. I was in the middle of the line, directly behind Ralph. Just as he went under the barbed wire, there was another flash of lightning. I was two or three feet away, but because of the rain pounding against my eyelids, I had trouble making out what happened. All I knew was that Ralph had stopped moving. I figured that he had been stunned, so I crawled past him under the fence. Once I was on the other side, I took hold of his arm and dragged him through.

I don't know how long we stayed in that field. An hour, I would guess, and the whole time we were there the rain and thunder and lightning continued to crash down upon us. It was a storm ripped from the pages of the Bible, and it went on and on and on, as if it would never end.

Two or three boys were hit by something—perhaps by lightning, perhaps by the shock of lightning as it struck the ground near them—and the meadow began to fill with their moans. Other boys wept and prayed. Still others, fear in their voices, tried to give sensible advice. Get rid of everything metal, they said, metal attracts the lightning. We all took off our belts and threw them away from us.

I don't remember saying anything. I don't remember crying. Another boy and I kept ourselves busy trying to take care of Ralph. He was still unconscious. We rubbed his hands and arms, we held down his tongue so he wouldn't swallow it, we told him to hang in there. After a while, his skin began to take on a bluish tinge. His body seemed colder to my touch, but in spite of the mounting evidence, it never once occurred to me that he wasn't going to come around. I was only fourteen years old, after all, and what did I know? I had never seen a dead person before.

It was the barbed wire that did it, I suppose. The other boys hit by the lightning went numb, felt pain in their limbs for an hour or so, and then recovered. But Ralph had been under the fence when the lightning struck, and he had been electrocuted on the spot.

Later on, when they told me he was dead, I learned that there was an eight-inch burn across his back. I remember trying to absorb this news and telling myself that life would never feel the same to me again. Strangely enough, I didn't think about how I had been right next to him when it happened. I didn't think, One or two seconds later, and it would have been me. What I thought about was holding his tongue and looking down at his teeth. His mouth had been set in a slight grimace, and with his lips partly open, I had spent an hour looking down at the tips of his teeth. Thirty-four years later, I still remember them. And his half-closed, half-open eyes. I remember those, too.

4

Not many years ago, I received a letter from a woman who lives in Brussels. In it, she told me the story of a friend of hers, a man she has known since childhood.

In 1940, this man joined the Belgian army. When the country fell to the Germans later that year, he was captured and put in a prisoner-of-war camp. He remained there until the war ended in 1945.

Prisoners were allowed to correspond with Red Cross workers back in Belgium. The man was arbitrarily assigned a pen pal—a Red Cross nurse from Brussels—and for the next five years he and this woman exchanged letters every month. Over the course of time they became fast friends. At a certain point (I'm not exactly sure how long this took), they understood that something more than friendship had developed between them. The correspondence went on, growing more intimate with each exchange, and at last they declared their love for each other. Was such a thing possible? They had never seen each other, had never spent a minute in each other's company.

After the war was over, the man was released from prison and returned to Brussels. He met the nurse, the nurse met him, and neither was disappointed. A short time later, they were married.

Years went by. They had children, they grew older, the world became a slightly different world. Their son completed his studies in Belgium and went off to do graduate work in Germany. At the university there, he fell in love with a young German woman. He wrote his parents and told them that he intended to marry her.

The parents on both sides couldn't have been happier for their children. The two families arranged to meet, and on the appointed day the German family showed up at the house of the Belgian family in Brussels. As the German father walked into the living room and the Belgian father rose to welcome him, the two men looked into each other's eyes and recognized each other. Many years had passed, but neither one was in any doubt as to who the other was. At one time in their lives, they had seen each other every day. The German father had been a guard in the prison camp where the Belgian father had spent the war.

As the woman who wrote me the letter hastened to add, there was no bad blood between them. However monstrous the German regime might have been, the German father had done nothing during those five years to turn the Belgian father against him.

Be that as it may, these two men are now the best of friends. The greatest joy in their lives is the grandchildren they have in common.

5

I was eight years old. At that moment in my life, nothing was more important to me than baseball. My team was the New York Giants, and I followed the doings of those men in the black-and-orange caps with all the devotion of a true believer. Even now, remembering that team which no longer exists, that played in a ballpark which no longer exists, I can reel off the names of nearly every player on the roster. Alvin Dark, Whitey Lockman, Don Mueller, Johnny Antonelli, Monte Irvin, Hoyt Wilhelm. But none was greater, none more perfect nor more deserving of worship than Willie Mays, the incandescent Say-Hey Kid.

That spring, I was taken to my first big-league game. Friends of my parents had box seats at the Polo Grounds, and one April night a group of us went to watch the Giants play the Milwaukee Braves. I don't know who won, I can't recall a single detail of the game, but I do remember that after the game was over my parents and their friends sat talking in their seats until all the other spectators had left. It got so late that we had to walk across the diamond and leave by the center-field exit, which was the only one still open. As it happened, that exit was right below the players' locker rooms.

Just as we approached the wall, I caught sight of Willie Mays. There was no question about who it was. It was Willie Mays, already out of uniform and standing there in his street clothes not ten feet away from me. I managed to keep my legs moving in his direction and then, mustering every ounce of my courage, I forced some words out of my mouth. "Mr. Mays," I said, "could I please have your autograph?"

He had to have been all of twenty-four years old, but I couldn't bring myself to pronounce his first name.

His response to my question was brusque but amiable. "Sure, kid, sure," he said. "You got a pencil?" He was so full of life, I remember, so full of youthful energy, that he kept bouncing up and down as he spoke.

I didn't have a pencil, so I asked my father if I could borrow his. He didn't have one either. Nor did my mother. Nor, as it turned out, did any of the other grown-ups.

The great Willie Mays stood there watching in silence. When it became clear that no one in the group had anything to write with, he turned to me and shrugged. "Sorry, kid," he said. "Ain't got no pencil, can't give no autograph." And then he walked out of the ballpark into the night.

I didn't want to cry, but tears started falling down my cheeks, and there was nothing I could do to stop them. Even worse, I cried all the way home in the car. Yes, I was crushed with disappointment, but I was also revolted at myself for not being able to control those tears. I wasn't a baby. I was eight years old, and big kids weren't supposed to cry over things like that. Not only did I not have Willie Mays's autograph, I didn't have anything else either. Life had put me to the test, and in all respects I had found myself wanting.

After that night, I started carrying a pencil with me wherever I went. It became a habit of mine never to leave the house without making sure I had a pencil in my pocket. It's not that I had any particular plans for that pencil, but I didn't want to be unprepared. I had been caught empty-handed once, and I wasn't about to let it happen again.

If nothing else, the years have taught me this: if there's a pencil in your pocket, there's a good chance that one day you'll feel tempted to start using it.

As I like to tell my children, that's how I became a writer.

1995

ACCIDENT REPORT

I

When A. was a young woman in San Francisco and just starting out in life, she went through a desperate period in which she almost lost her mind. In the space of just a few weeks, she was fired from her job, one of her best friends was murdered when thieves broke into her apartment at night, and A.'s beloved cat became seriously ill. I don't know the exact nature of the illness, but it was apparently life-threatening, and when A. took the cat to the vet, he told her that the cat would die within a month unless a certain operation was performed. She asked him how much the operation would cost. He toted up the various charges for her, and the amount came to three hundred twenty-seven dollars. A. didn't have that kind of money. Her bank account was down to almost zero, and for the next several days she walked around in a state of extreme distress, alternately thinking about her dead friend and the impossible sum needed to prevent her cat from dying: three hundred twenty-seven dollars.

One day, she was driving through the Mission and came to a stop at a red light. Her body was there, but her thoughts were somewhere else, and in the gap between them, in that small space that no one has fully explored but where we all sometimes live, she heard the voice of her murdered friend. *Don't worry*, the voice said. *Don't worry. Things will get better soon.* The light turned green, but A. was still under the spell of this auditory hallucination, and she did not move. A moment later, a car rammed into her from behind, breaking one of the taillights and crumpling the fender. The man who was driving that car shut off his engine, climbed out of the car, and walked over to A. He apologized for doing such a stupid thing. No, A. said, it was my fault. The light turned green and I didn't go. But the man insisted that he was the one to blame. When he learned that A. didn't have collision insurance (she was too poor for luxuries like that), he offered to pay for any damages that had been done to her car. Get an estimate on what it will cost, he said, and send me the bill. My insurance company will take care of it. A. continued to protest, telling the man that he wasn't responsible for the accident, but he wouldn't take no for an answer, and finally she gave in. She took the car to a garage and asked the mechanic to assess the costs of repairing the fender and the taillight. When she returned several hours later, he handed her a written estimate. Give or take a penny or two, the amount came to exactly three hundred twenty-seven dollars.

2

_____

W., the friend from San Francisco who told me that story, has been directing films for twenty years. His latest project is based on a novel that recounts the adventures of a mother and her teenage daughter. It is a work of fiction, but most of the events in the book are taken directly from the author's life. The author, now a grown woman, was once the teenage daughter, and the mother in the story—who is still alive—was her real mother.

W.'s film was shot in Los Angeles. A famous actress was hired to play the role of the mother, and according to what W. told me on a recent visit to New York, the filming went smoothly and the production was completed on schedule. Once he began to edit the movie, however, he decided that he wanted to add a few more scenes, which he felt would greatly enhance the story. One of them included a shot of the mother parking her car on a street in a residential neighborhood. The location manager went out scouting for an appropriate street, and eventually one was chosen—

arbitrarily, it would seem, since one Los Angeles street looks more or less like any other. On the appointed morning, W., the actress, and the film crew gathered on the street to shoot the scene. The car that the actress was supposed to drive was parked in front of a house—no particular house, just one of the houses on that street—and as my friend and his leading lady stood on the sidewalk discussing the scene and the possible ways to approach it, the door of that house burst open and a woman came running out. She appeared to be laughing and screaming at the same time. Distracted by the commotion, W. and the actress stopped talking. A screaming and laughing woman was running across the front lawn, and she was headed straight for them. I don't know how big the lawn was. W. neglected to mention that detail when he told the story, but in my mind I see it as large, which would have given the woman a considerable distance to cover before she reached the sidewalk and announced who she was. A moment like that deserves to be prolonged, it seems to me—if only by a few seconds—for the thing that was about to happen was so improbable, so outlandish in its defiance of the odds, that one wants to savor it for a few extra seconds before letting go of it. The woman running across the lawn was the novelist's mother. A fictional character in her daughter's book, she was also her real mother, and now, by pure accident, she was about to meet the woman who was playing that fictional character in a film based on the book in which her character had in fact been herself. She was real, but she was also imaginary. And the actress who was playing her was both real and imaginary as well. There were two of them standing on the sidewalk that morning, but there was also just one. Or perhaps it was the same one twice. According to what my friend told me, when the women finally understood what had happened, they threw their arms around each other and embraced.

3

Last September, I had to go to Paris for a few days, and my publisher booked a room for me in a small hotel on the Left Bank. It's the same hotel they use for all their authors, and I had already stayed there several times in the past. Other than its convenient location—midway down a narrow street just off the Boulevard Saint-Germain—there is nothing even remotely interesting about this hotel. Its rates are modest, its rooms are cramped, and it is not mentioned in any guidebook. The people who run it are pleasant enough, but it is no more than a drab and inconspicuous hole-in-the-wall, and except for a couple of American writers who have the same French publisher I do, I have never met anyone who has stayed there. I mention this fact because the obscurity of the hotel plays a part in the story. Unless one stops for a moment to consider how many hotels there are in Paris (which attracts more visitors than any other city in the world) and then further considers how many rooms there are in those hotels (thousands, no doubt tens of thousands), the full import of what happened to me last year will not be understood.

I arrived at the hotel late—more than an hour behind schedule—and checked in at the front desk. I went upstairs immediately after that. Just as I was putting my key into the door of my room, the telephone started to ring. I went in, tossed my bag on the floor, and picked up the phone, which was set into a nook in the wall just beside the bed, more or less at pillow level. Because the phone was turned in toward the bed, and because the cord was short, and because the one chair in the room was out of reach, it was necessary to sit down on the bed in order to use the phone. That's what I did, and as I talked to the person on the other end of the line, I noticed a piece of paper lying under the desk on the opposite side of the room. If I had been anywhere else, I wouldn't have been in a position to see it. The dimensions of the room were so tight that the space between the desk and the foot of the bed was no more than four or five feet. From my vantage point at the head of the bed, I was in the only place that provided a low enough angle of the floor to see what was under the desk. After the conversation was over, I got off the bed, crouched down under the desk, and picked up the piece of paper.

Curious, of course, always curious, but not at all expecting to find anything out of the ordinary. The paper turned out to be one of those little message forms they slip under your door in European hotels. To——and From——, the date and the time, and then a blank square below for the message. The form had been folded in three, and printed out in block letters on the outer fold was the name of one of my closest friends. We don't see each other often (O. lives in Canada), but we have been through a number of memorable experiences together, and there has never been anything but the greatest affection between us. Seeing his name on the message form made me very happy. We hadn't spoken in a while, and I had had no inkling that he would be in Paris when I was there. In those first moments of discovery and incomprehension, I assumed that O. had somehow gotten wind of the fact that I was coming and had called the hotel to leave a message for me. The message had been delivered to my room, but whoever had brought it up had placed it carelessly on the edge of the desk, and it had blown onto the floor. Or else that person had accidentally dropped it (the chambermaid?) while preparing the room for my arrival. One way or the other, neither explanation was very plausible. The angle was wrong, and unless someone had kicked the message after it had fallen to the floor, the paper couldn't have been lying so far under the desk. I was already beginning to reconsider my hypothesis when something more important occurred to me. O.'s name was on the outside of the message form. If the message had been meant for me, my name would have been there. The recipient was the one whose name belonged on the outside, not the sender, and if my name wasn't there, it surely wasn't going to be anywhere else. I opened the message and read it. The sender was someone I had never heard of—but the recipient was indeed O. I rushed downstairs and asked the clerk at the front desk if O. was still there. It was a stupid question, of course, but I asked it anyway. How could O. be there if he was no longer in his room? I was there now, and O.'s room was no longer his room but mine. I asked the clerk when he had checked out. An hour ago, the clerk said. An hour ago I had been sitting in a taxi at the edge of Paris, stuck in a traffic jam. If I had made it to the hotel at the expected time, I would have run into O. just as he was walking out the door.

1999

IT DON'T MEAN A THING

I

We used to see him occasionally at the Carlyle Hotel. It would be an exaggeration to call him a friend, but F. was a good acquaintance, and my wife and I always looked forward to his arrival when he called to say that he was coming to town. A daring and prolific French poet, F. was also one of the world's leading authorities on Henri Matisse. So great was his reputation, in fact, that an important French museum asked him to organize a large exhibition of Matisse's work. F. wasn't a professional curator, but he threw himself into the job with enormous energy and skill. The idea was to gather together all of Matisse's paintings from a particular five-year period in the middle of his career. Dozens of canvases were involved, and since they were scattered around in private collections and museums all over the world, it took F. several years to prepare the show. In the end, there was only one work that could not be found—but it was a crucial one, the centerpiece of the entire exhibition. F. had not been able to track down the owner, had no idea where it was, and without that canvas years of travel and meticulous labor would go for naught. For the next six months, he devoted himself exclusively to the search for that one painting, and when he found it, he realized that it had been no more than a few feet away from him the whole time. The owner was a woman who lived in an apartment at the Carlyle Hotel. The Carlyle was F.'s hotel of choice, and he stayed there whenever he was in New York. More than that, the woman's apartment was located directly above the room that F. always reserved for himself—just one floor up. Which meant that every time F. had gone to sleep at the Carlyle Hotel, wondering where the missing painting could have been, it had been hanging on a wall directly above his head. Like an image from a dream.

2

I wrote that paragraph last October. A few days later, a friend from Boston called to tell me that a poet acquaintance of his was in bad shape. In his mid-sixties now, this man has spent his life in the far reaches of the literary solar system—the single inhabitant of an asteroid that orbits around a tertiary moon of Pluto, visible only through the strongest telescope. I have never met him, but I have read his work, and I have always imagined him living on his small planet like some latter-day Little Prince.

My friend told me that the poet's health was in decline. He was undergoing treatments for his illness, his money was at a low ebb, and he was being threatened with eviction from his apartment. As a way to raise some quick and necessary cash to rescue the poet from his troubles, my friend had come up with the idea of producing a book in his honor. He would solicit contributions from several dozen poets and writers, gather them into an attractive, limited-edition volume, and sell the copies by subscription only. He figured there were enough book collectors in the country to guarantee a handsome profit. Once the money came in, it would all be turned over to the sick and struggling poet.

He asked me if I had a page or two lying around somewhere that I might give him, and I mentioned the little story I had just written about my French friend and the missing painting. I faxed it to him that same morning, and a few hours later he called back to say that he liked the piece and wanted to include it in the book. I was glad to have done my little bit, and then, once the matter had been settled, I promptly forgot all about it.

Two nights ago (January 31, 2000), I was sitting with my twelve-year-old daughter at the dining room table in our house in Brooklyn, helping her with her math homework—a massive list of problems involving negative and positive numbers. My daughter is not terribly interested in math, and once we finished converting the subtractions into additions and the negatives into positives, we started talking about the music recital that had been held at her school several nights before. She had sung "The First Time Ever I Saw Your Face," the old Roberta Flack number, and now she was looking for another song to begin preparing for the spring recital. After tossing some ideas back and forth, we both decided that she should do something bouncy and up-tempo this time, in contrast to the slow and aching ballad she had just performed. Without any warning, she sprang from her chair and began belting out the lyrics of "It Don't Mean a Thing if it Ain't Got that Swing." I know that parents tend to exaggerate the talents of their children, but there was no question in my mind that her rendition of that song was remarkable. Dancing and shimmying as the music poured out of her, she took her voice to places it had rarely been before, and because she sensed that herself, could feel the power of her own performance, she immediately launched into it again after she had finished. Then she sang it again. And then again. For fifteen or twenty minutes, the house was filled with increasingly beautiful and ecstatic variations of a single unforgettable phrase: *It don't mean a thing if it ain't got that swing.*

The following afternoon (yesterday), I brought in the mail at around two o'clock. There was a considerable pile of it, the usual mixture of junk and important business. One letter had been sent by a small New York poetry publisher, and I opened that one first. Unexpectedly, it contained the proofs of my contribution to my friend's book. I read through the piece again, making one or two corrections, and then called the copy editor responsible for the production of the book. Her name and number had been provided in a cover letter sent by the publisher, and once we had had our brief chat, I hung up the phone and turned to the rest of my mail. Wedged inside the pages of my daughter's new issue of *Seventeen Magazine*, there was a slim white package that had been sent from France. When I turned it over to look at the return address, I saw that it was from F., the same poet whose experience with the missing painting had inspired me to write the short piece I had just read over for the first time since composing it in October. What a coincidence, I thought. My life has been filled with dozens of curious events like this one, and no matter how hard I try, I can't seem to shake free of them. What is it about the world that continues to involve me in such nonsense?

Then I opened the package. There was a thin book of poetry inside—what we would refer to as a chapbook; what the French call a *plaquette*. It was just thirty-two pages long, and it had been printed on fine, elegant paper. As I flipped through it, scanning a phrase here and a phrase there, immediately recognizing the exuberant and frenetic style that characterizes all of F.'s work, a tiny slip of paper fell out of the book and fluttered onto my desk. It was no more than two inches long and half an inch high. I had no idea what it was. I had never encountered a stray slip of paper in a new book before, and unless it was supposed to serve as some kind of rarefied, microscopic bookmark to match the refinement of the book itself, it seemed to have been put in there by mistake. I picked up the errant rectangle from my desk, turned it over, and saw that there was writing on the other side—eleven short words arranged in a single row of type. The poems had been written in French, the book had been printed in France, but the words on the slip of paper that had fallen out of the book were in English. They formed a sentence, and that sentence read: *It don't mean a thing if it ain't got that swing.*

3

Having come this far, I can't resist the temptation to add one more link to this chain of anecdotes. As I was writing the last words of the first paragraph in the second section printed above ("living on his small planet like some latter-day Little Prince"), I was reminded of the fact that *The Little Prince* was written in New York. Few people know this, but after Saint-Exupéry was demobilized following the French defeat in 1940, he came to America, and for a time he lived at 240 Central Park South in Manhattan. It was there that he wrote his celebrated book, the most French of all French children's books. *Le Petit Prince* is required reading for nearly every American high school student of French, and as was the case with so many others before me, it was the first book I happened to read in a language that wasn't English. I went on to read more books in French. Eventually, I translated French books as a way of earning my living as a young man, and at a certain point I lived in France for four years. That was where I first met F. and became familiar with his work. It might be an outlandish statement, but I believe it is safe to say that if I hadn't read *Le Petit Prince* as an adolescent in 1963, I never would have been in a position to receive F.'s book in the mail thirty-seven years later. In saying that, I am also saying that I never would have discovered the mysterious slip of paper bearing the words *It don't mean a thing if it ain't got that swing.*

240 Central Park South is an odd, misshapen building that stands on the corner overlooking Columbus Circle. Construction was completed in 1941, and the first tenants moved in just before Pearl Harbor and America's entrance into the war. I don't know the exact date when Saint-Exupéry took up residence there, but he had to have been among the first people to live in that building. By one of those curious anomalies that mean absolutely nothing, so was my mother. She moved there from Brooklyn with her parents and sister at the age of sixteen, and she did not move out until she married my father five years later. It was an extraordinary step for the family to take—from Crown Heights to one of the most elegant addresses in Manhattan—and it moves me to think that my mother lived in the same building where Saint-Exupéry wrote *The Little Prince.* If nothing else, I am moved by the fact that she had no idea that the book was being written, no idea who the author was. Nor did she have any

knowledge of his death some time later when his plane went down in the last year of the war. Around that same time, my mother fell in love with an aviator. As it happened, he, too, died in that same war.

My grandparents went on living at 240 Central Park South until their deaths (my grandmother in 1968; my grandfather in 1979), and many of my most important childhood memories are situated in their apartment. My mother moved to New Jersey after she married my father, and we changed houses several times during my early years, but the New York apartment was always there, a fixed point in an otherwise unstable universe. It was there that I stood at the window and watched the traffic swirling around the statue of Christopher Columbus. It was there that my grandfather performed his magic tricks for me. It was there that I came to understand that New York was my city.

Just as my mother had done, her sister moved out of the apartment when she married. Not long after that (in the early fifties), she and her husband moved to Europe, where they lived for the next twelve years. In thinking about the various decisions I have made in my own life, I have no doubt that their example inspired me to move to France when I was in my early twenties. When my aunt and uncle returned to New York, my young cousin was eleven years old. I had met him only once. His parents sent him to school at the French lycée, and because of the incongruities in our respective educations, we wound up reading *Le Petit Prince* at the same time, even though there was a six-year difference in our ages. Back then, neither one of us knew that the book had been written in the same building where our mothers had lived.

After their return from Europe, my cousin and his parents settled into an apartment on the Upper East Side. For the next several years, he had his hair cut every month at the barbershop in the Carlyle Hotel.

2000